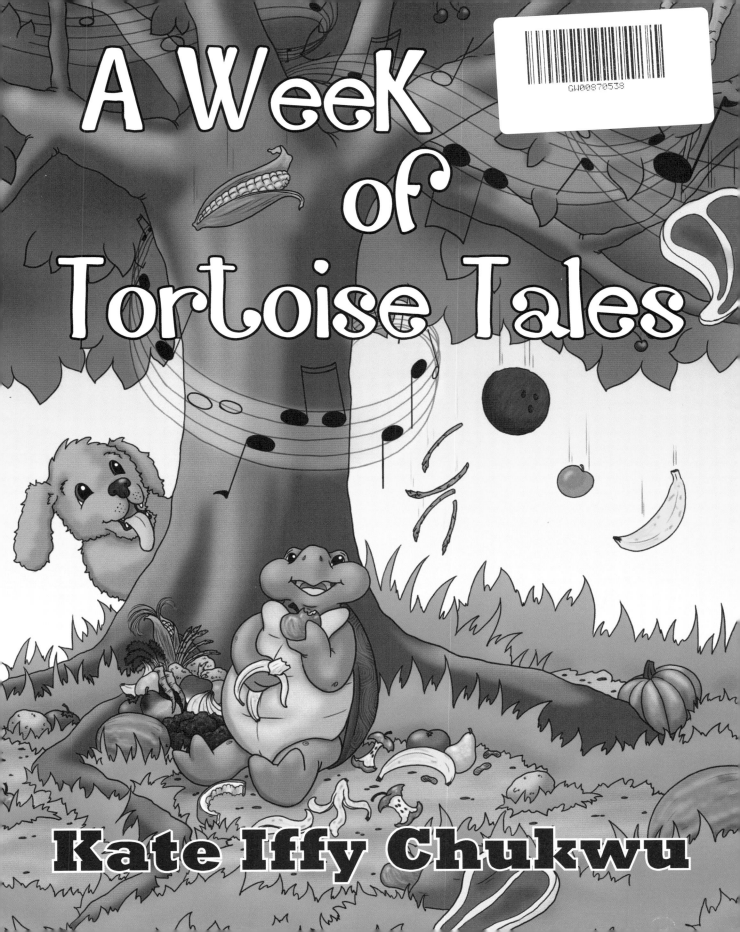

A Week of Tortoise Tales

Kate Iffy Chukwu

A WeeK of Tortoise Tales

Kate Iffy Chukwu

To Bradley, Jessica, Isabel and Chinua.

Thanks for inspiring me to write these stories.

Contents

About This Book

For many years, tortoise tales lived
in the memories of grandparents, aunts, uncles,
mothers, fathers, and teachers. When each person
told a particular story, they added bits or left out bits
to suit their audience. Because of this, the stories have
changed over the years. Today, there are many different
versions.

My grandmother was a beautiful storyteller. I clearly
remember her stories about the tortoise as well as
other animals. Her stories always showed the tortoise
as being clever, greedy, silly, or tricky. Sometimes, he
got away with his silly pranks, other times he didn't. My

grandmother told these stories mostly at night, taking us to spectacular worlds where a tortoise could sing, take part in a race, cook, fly, and even get married! All tortoise tales had great lessons to be learned.

In *A Week of Tortoise Tales,* I have kept to the oral tradition of storytelling while also making it relevant for modern young readers and listeners. Older children will find the tales fascinating. Parents and grandparents will also find the tales appealing to share with children of *all* ages. These short and simple tales are just right for everyone.

Go on then, get started.

Each story is about five minutes of fun!

Monday

Flying Lessons

It was a Monday morning and Tortoise was bored. He wanted to do something exciting. He decided to see King Koboh.

"I want to be your Special Adviser," he said to the king, beaming.

"Why?" asked King Koboh.

"I'm the cleverest and the finest animal," said Tortoise, admiring his smooth, glossy back in a mirror.

But King Koboh wasn't so sure. Just then he saw a bird flying outside his window.

"If you're the cleverest animal, fly like that bird by noon tomorrow."

"But…Sir, I'm not a bird," said Tortoise with a gasp.

King Koboh pointed at the door.

"Out!"

"Nooooo!" howled Tortoise.

If I disobey him, thought Tortoise, *he could have me locked in jail.* Tortoise went pale. He had to fly. But how?

Suddenly, he had a clever idea. Eagle could teach him how to fly.

"Great friend, I'm in big trouble," he cried as soon as he got to her house.

"What is it?" asked Eagle.

Tortoise told her all about King Koboh's order. "Please, dear friend, teach me how to fly."

"What? You haven't even got wings," squeaked Eagle.

"I know," whispered Tortoise.

There was a long moment of silence before Eagle shouted,

"Aha, I've got an idea!"

"I'm usually the one with ideas!" said Tortoise.

"Shut up for once!" said Eagle, flapping her wings. "I'll carry you on my back and we will fly over the palace."

"How?" asked Tortoise.

"Let's practice," she said. "Climb on my back. Now, hold on to my feathers with your mouth."

As soon as Tortoise was steady, the large bird spread out her wings. Up and up and up she flew. She floated. She swooped, round and round in circles. Poor Tortoise felt sick.

"Oh dear," he said, as soon as they landed.

Tortoise went straight home to bed with a headache. Luckily, the next day he felt better. He was ready to fly.

"Thanks for everything," he told Eagle.

"It's really no bother," she replied. "Aha! I've just remembered. You must shut your mouth while we fly, otherwise you'll fall. Can you do that?"

"Easy peasy." Tortoise smiled.

He climbed on his friend's back. He held her feathers in his mouth. Away they went. Up and up and up they flew. They floated. They swooped, round and round in circles.

Tortoise couldn't believe his eyes. He saw the hills, the valleys, the rivers, the lakes, the trees, and the forest. *So much fresh air*, he thought.

Then Eagle flew a little slower. They were close to the palace. King Koboh was sitting in the garden. He saw the strange shape high in the air.

"It's…it's…Tortoise!" he screamed. "He's flying!"

"Tortoise—" shouted King Koboh, "—you *are* the cleverest!"

"I told—" but no one knew what Tortoise was going to say. He had opened his mouth and lost his grip on Eagle.

"AAAAAAAARRRRRHHHHHHHHHHHHHH!"

He tumbled down, down, down from the sky.

Crash! Smash!

He landed right in the middle of an empty pond. Eagle gasped. King Koboh gaped. Tortoise was lying upside down. He looked like he was in pain. His once smooth, glossy shell was in pieces all around him.

"Oh dear," Eagle said.

She flew off quickly and came back with her friends. Together, they picked him up. They used sap from a tree to glue the pieces of his broken shell back together again.

Tortoise was all right, but after his mighty fall, he began to do things very slowly and carefully.

Now, he can be seen walking about slowly with a shell that looks like a jigsaw puzzle.

Tuesday

Sizzling Stew

One very hot Tuesday afternoon, Tortoise was very hungry. He went out to look for food. *Not even a worm-infested mango around*, he thought.

Just then, Goat staggered round a tree, pulling something very heavy. He was surprised to see Tortoise.

"What are you doing near my house?" he asked.

"Um, I was just hanging out," said Tortoise, hoping Goat didn't know he was lying.

"Why don't you come in for some food? Later, we can open this treasure chest!" Goat smiled.

Food! He quivered. *I would gobble and guzzle and stuff my face.*

"Oh, all right, but make it snappy," said Tortoise, trying to disguise his desire.

Goat made some sizzling spicy stew. Instead of dishing out the food, he began to talk about the treasure chest. The tempting smell of delicious stew drifted into Tortoise's nose. His mouth began to water.

But Goat talked and talked and *talked*. And Tortoise waited and waited and *waited*. The aroma was so tempting he couldn't wait any longer. Finally, he had a clever idea.

"Monkey offered to give you lots of fresh green leaves and hay," said Tortoise. "You should go and thank him before he changes his mind."

"Great! I'll be back in a jiffy!" said Goat. He hurried off to see Monkey.

Tip toe. Tip toe. Tortoise slipped into the kitchen. Slowly, carefully, he opened the pot. He looked to the left. He looked to the right. The coast was clear. He tasted the stew.

"Yummy, yummy." He smiled and wiped his oily mouth.

Then he heard a sound. He waited and listened. It wasn't Goat; it was just the whistling wind. He ate some more. He gobbled and guzzled and stuffed his face. He knew Goat would be back any minute, because Monkey wasn't even in town.

Tortoise looked into the pot. *Oops. I've eaten quite a big portion. Goat would be furious. Should I run away?* he thought.

He put some sizzling stew in his hat and crept outside. Suddenly, Goat appeared. Tortoise was confused. He put on his hat immediately.

"Sorry I kept you," Goat told him. "I waited at Monkey's house, but he never showed up."

"It's all right. I'll be off now," said Tortoise in a shaky voice.

"So soon?" asked Goat.

"Yessss," replied Tortoise. The food was becoming too hot for his head. He winced.

"What about lunch?" Goat asked.

"Another time." Tortoise groaned.

"Are you upset with me?" asked Goat.

"Yes…I mean, no. I'm in a terrible hurry," said Tortoise. He was beginning to feel really uncomfortable.

"You're sweating. Do you have a fever?" asked Goat.

"Um, a little," said Tortoise.

Oh, if only Goat would get out of my way!

"Do you need some medicine?" asked Goat.

"No, thank you!" bellowed Tortoise. He felt a trickle behind his ears.

"I can give you—"

"For goodness sake, don't bother!" Tortoise was getting angry.

"I really don't mind," said Goat.

Tortoise was now really angry. He couldn't think of a way to get Goat to leave him alone. The pain had become unbearable.

"AAARRGGHHHHHH!!!"

Tortoise shrieked and took off his hat. The food fell out, followed by all of his hair.

"Ow!" screamed Goat, staring at Tortoise head, which was now bald with a bit of stew.

Tortoise gasped. His hair was on the floor and his head was sore. *How could I be so foolish? I will never ever steal again. Oh my hair! Will it ever grow back? he thought.*

But, it never did. That is why Tortoise is now bald.

Wednesday

Hot Competition

It was a Wednesday morning and Tortoise woke up feeling very sad. His cousin was wedding soon and he had no money to buy a good outfit. The other day, he asked some of the animals for money.

"Give me a teeny-weeny amount. I'll pay you back," he begged.

"No way!" said Pig. "You borrowed one bag of money and you haven't paid back."

"But …"

"No way!" said Rabbit. "You borrowed two jars of honey and you haven't paid back."

"But …"

"No way!" said Hippo. "You borrowed three bags of munchies and you haven't paid back.

"But…"

The animals walked away and refused to lend him any money. Now he was stuck—no money, no outfit, no wedding.

And then he had a clever idea. It was so clever, that he couldn't believe he hadn't thought of it before. He would visit the next town over and borrow some money. Strangers would never know that he wouldn't pay them back!

That afternoon, he travelled to the next town. He noticed that both animals and humans were arguing.

"I'll win!" shrieked Elephant.

"You won't!" said Man.

"Win? Win what?" asked Tortoise.

"Haven't you heard about the competition and the winner's money?" asked Antelope.

Money? Had he heard the word *money*? His outfit, his cousin's wedding, *everything* cost money.

Tortoise smiled.

"Welcome to The Boiling Water Competition," announced their leader. "These are the rules. You must drink this cup of boiling water *without* spitting it out on the ground. The winner gets a bag of money!"

Antelope went first. "I've just finished a race and I'm quite thirsty," he beamed. Then, he took a gulp.

"URGH!" he screamed, spitting the water out. He was out of the competition.

Elephant was next. "With my size, this shouldn't be a problem," he boasted. Then, he took a gulp.

"ARGH!" he yelled, spitting the water out. He too, was out of the competition.

One by one, the crowd tried. They all failed. Tortoise went last. He needed enough time to come up with a clever idea. He held the cup of boiling water. He could feel the hot steam covering his face.

"Great leader, can I say something please?" he begged.

"All right," the leader replied.

Tortoise cleared his throat. He began to speak very slowly. "Thank you for the terrific, wonderful, and extraordinary opportunity you've given me to enter this marvellous, tremendous, and grand competition."

"You're welcome," the leader said. "Now, go ahead."

"Before I drink this, I'd like to sing a song of praise to you," said Tortoise.

The leader nodded. He loved to hear how great he was. Soon, Tortoise taught everyone how to sing the chorus to his quickly-made-up song.

"Aha! Please sing loudly," he reminded them.

"*Oh…oh…lovely leader, live forever!*" he sang.

Everyone, including him, responded, "*Whewhow, whewhow, whewhow.*"

They kept on singing and singing.

Unknown to them, Tortoise was just being clever and tricky. The louder they sang, the easier it was for him to blow cool air inside the cup of boiling water. After some time, the song ended.

"I'm ready to drink!" He bowed.

First, he took a sip, then a gulp. He began to drink the water, which of course, was no longer hot. When he had finished, he turned the cup upside down for everyone to see.

"Yay!" everyone cheered.

The leader handed him the bag of money.

Tortoise screamed with joy. He thought about all the things he would buy for the wedding—a suit, sunshades, a nice hat— but then he stopped and listened.

"He sang a long boring song," moaned Elephant.

"And wasted so much time," Antelope muttered.

Man scratched his chin and shook his head.

Up the path, down the path, across the road, down the hill, and through the forest, Tortoise hurried back home before anyone discovered his trick.

From that day onwards, Tortoise realised that even though he was small, he could play some really cool tricks on bigger animals. Mind you, he doesn't always get away with it.

Questions

Monday – Flying Lessons

1. Tortoise had a difficult task. What's the most difficult thing you ever did?

2. Do you think it was fair or unfair of King Koboh to make such an order? Why?

3. How did Eagle behave in this story?

4. What's the kindest thing you ever did?

Tuesday – Sizzling Stew

1. If someone stole something that belonged to you, what would you do if you caught the person?

2. If you were Tortoise and you met Goat the next day, what might you say to him?

3. Have you ever helped a friend? What did you do?

4. If Tortoise said, "I've learnt an important lesson today," what would that lesson be?

Wednesday – Hot Competition

1. Tortoise needed money. When have you needed something so desperately? What did you do about it? Did you get it?

2. Have you ever played a cool trick on someone older or bigger than you? What did you do?

3. Do you think it was fair or unfair of Tortoise to win the competition?

4. How would you have wanted this story to end?

Thursday

Common Sense

One late Thursday afternoon,

Tortoise decided he was going to play *no more tricks!* He thought instead about having all the common sense there was in the world. He would be the wisest animal. He knew animals and humans alike would pay him lots of money to solve their problems. He would become rich.

Tortoise first travelled North, then East, then South, then West, looking everywhere for common sense.

He crept around.

Sneak, sneak.

He hid and listened to people.

Peep, peep. After a long while, he found *so* much of it.

There couldn't possibly be any more common sense in the world, he thought. He gathered all of it in a big pot made from the finest clay. He covered the top tightly with a strong material so that none of the common sense could escape.

"Now, I'm the wisest." He chuckled and rubbed his hands with joy.

Tortoise wanted to tell everyone about his newfound wisdom. But then he thought, *Animals! They could steal my pot. They could even become wiser than me. I better hide this pot somewhere safe.*

That evening, Tortoise found a cave. "Too dark and cold." He shuddered.

He walked to the river. "Too wet and deep." He sighed.

On his way back home, he walked past a tall palm tree. That's when he had a clever idea. He looked up the top branches. *Aha!* The best hiding spot!

Tortoise hung the pot on his belly with a rope. He climbed the tree, but the pot was in his way. He climbed down and tried again. Climbing the tree wasn't easy. The pot kept getting stuck.

He climbed again.

"ARGH!" screeched Tortoise. He climbed down, huffing and puffing.

Ant, who was busy as usual, noticed what had been going on. He burst out laughing.

"Foolish Tortoise," he said. "You can't climb a palm tree like that! Get a stronger rope and tie it around yourself and the tree."

Tortoise sighed.

"I've seen many palm wine tappers do that," added Ant. "Don't forget to put the pot behind

you, otherwise you'll be here for a hundred years or more!"

Tortoise did exactly what Ant suggested. It was much easier. This time, he climbed higher and higher until he was right at the top.

"It worked!" shouted Ant from the ground. "By the way, what's in your pot?"

"All the common sense in the world," replied Tortoise.

"Ha ha ha ha ha! Did you say common sense?" asked Ant. "*Use* it next time!"

Tortoise felt embarrassed. He thought he had collected all the common sense there was and yet here was tiny Ant with so much of it! He could still hear Ant giggling. He became furious. He grabbed the pot and flung it hard at Ant, who had already stepped aside. The pot hit the bottom of the tree and smashed into many pieces. All the common sense spilled out.

"Noooooo!" wailed Tortoise when he climbed down. Soon, a mighty wind began to blow and scattered the common sense all over the world. Human beings and animals everywhere got some of it or just a little. Tortoise collected the common sense that had blown across his face and went back home. That is why sometimes Tortoise is wise. Other times, he is very foolish.

Friday

Silly Princesses

On a Friday afternoon, there was another competition. It was a competition of cleverness—anyone who found out the name of a princess was worthy of marrying her. The Queen was the only one in the entire kingdom who knew the names of her daughters.

"My middle name is *Clever*," boasted Tortoise, looking at the poster.

"But you're not *worthy*," said Rhino. "You're just an animal."

"Thanks for reminding me," said Tortoise.

Beautiful princess, magnificent palace, free massages, free food…more free food. He sighed. Tortoise spent the whole night dreaming about food.

The next morning, he waited outside the huge palace gates just in time to see the princesses' step out for their usual walk.

"Hello, lovely ladies," he said, waving some money at them. "I'll soon be travelling to London, Los Angeles, and Lagos. If you tell me your names, I'll take you with me."

"Ewww!" the princesses squealed together and hurried off.

Silly billies! thought Tortoise. *How could they treat me like rotten bananas?*

Tortoise spent the rest of the day thinking. He spent that night thinking. By morning, he had a clever idea.

Everyone knew the princesses loved cherries. So, Tortoise got lots of them and put them in a transparent container in front of the palace gate. He then hid behind a tree.

As soon as the princesses stepped out for their usual walk, they noticed the red fruits.

"This must be a gift from a kind person," said one of the princesses, popping one in her mouth.

"Yay, fresh cherries!" another said, stuffing two in her mouth.

Gobble! Munch!

"Yummy!" said the youngest, stuffing three in her mouth.

Munch, munch, munch!

In no time, all the cherries were gone. Tortoise rushed out of his hiding place.

"No, no, no, no, no, *no!*" he cried, pointing to the empty container.

"What is it?" one of them asked.

"My cherries!" yelled Tortoise. "They were for my sick mother. The doctor said only cherries would make her better," Tortoise cried, with fake tears.

The princesses began to cry.

"Mimi saw the fruits first." The youngest one pointed at a sister.

"That's unfair, Sisi!" shouted Mimi. "Didi gobbled one first!"

"That's ridiculous!" snapped Didi. "Kiki gave one to me!"

"We are *so* sorry," said Kiki.

"It's all right," said Tortoise, wiping his fake tears. "I'll try to get Mama some more."

Whoopee! He knew their names at last!

That Friday afternoon, the day of the competition, news had reached the palace that someone was ready to announce the name of a princess. The palace was packed.

"It must be a handsome prince," some whispered.

"And a clever one too," some said.

The palace fell silent.

"May the clever and worthy man step forward with a name please," the Queen said proudly.

Tortoise stepped out.

Ho, ho, ho, ha, ha, ha!

Everyone roared with laughter. The Queen laughed so hard that her crown wobbled.

Tortoise took a bow. Then he did a little tap dance. "I'm ready," he said.

"Go ahead." The Queen chuckled. She was sure Tortoise would never know the names of her daughters.

"The names of my soon-to-be wives are Didi, Mimi, Kiki, and Sisi," said Tortoise.

"W-what?" the Queen asked, stumbling over her words.

The princesses gasped.

'tap dance'

Everyone stared. No one was sure the names were right.

The princesses screamed. They ran to their mother, the Queen.

"Mother, please!" Didi cried. "Tortoise can't be our husband. He's not even a man."

But the Queen wouldn't go back on her word. She allowed Tortoise marry all four of her daughters, though it made her sad.

Tortoise whooped with joy. His brilliant trick had paid off. *Free food, nice home, here I come*! he thought as he hopped around like a grasshopper on the dance floor.

From that day onwards, Tortoise has enjoyed living in environments where he is handled with care, well fed and kept clean.

Questions

Thursday – Common Sense

1. Do you think it was a good or bad idea for Tortoise to hide all the common sense in the world? Why?

2. What would you do if someone ever laughs at you?

3. What have you ever tried to do, over and over again, and somehow it wasn't working?

4. What's the most embarrassing thing that ever happened to you?

Friday – Silly Princesses

1. What competition have you ever been in? Did you win? Why?

2. How many cherries can you stuff in your mouth?

3. If the Queen said, "I've learnt an important lesson," what would that lesson be?

4. How would you have wanted this story to end?

Saturday

The Magic Tree

Tortoise's cheeks were the size of two ripe oranges. Other animals were starving and getting thinner, but Tortoise was getting fatter and fatter.

"Tell us your secret," begged his friends.

He wouldn't tell them about the magic tree. The animals could finish the food and he could be left with nothing.

Each day Tortoise sang to the tree:

Oh, magnificent tree, send down food quickly.

My wife and kids are starving terribly,

so send down anything, anything at all

The tree would move its branches in pity and all types of delicious, mouth-watering food and fruits would come showering down.

Gobble, gobble! Chomp, chomp! Munch, munch!

Tortoise never took any food home to his wife or kids. He ate until his belly almost burst. He even managed to squeeze in some mangoes for pudding! *Yum, yum!*

One Saturday afternoon, Dog was digging soil beside the magic tree. He didn't know the tree did any sort of magic. Just then, he heard something. He peeped. Tortoise was singing.

As he sang, the branches began to shake. Lots of food began to fall from the tree. Dog had never seen anything like that.

Look at those ripe fresh juicy fruits! thought Dog. He whistled.

"Who's there?" asked Tortoise.

"It's only me," said Dog. "Oh, teach me your song. Please. Oh, please."

Tortoise considered. "If I teach you, you must promise to say nothing about what you've seen here today."

"*I promise!*" shrieked Dog.

Tortoise taught him the magic song. Lots of delicious food came showering down again. Dog munched and crunched and guzzled and gobbled. He even had melons and banana for dessert! *Yippee!*

But Dog couldn't keep a secret. He told the rest of the animals. In no time, they gathered under the magic tree.

"Do you remember the song?" Lion asked Dog.

"Sure," said Dog, and he began to sing. Suddenly, the tree began to shower all kinds of food. The animals were amazed. They were pushing and shoving, grabbing and pouncing, clawing and gobbling, until there was no more food on the ground.

"Sing, Dog, sing!" the animals demanded, again and again. Dog sang and sang and the tree kept showering down food. Soon, however, it stopped. The animals went home with wide smiles on their faces.

Now the tree was very angry. It had no more food left.

The next day, Tortoise went as usual and sang to the tree. To his surprise, all sizes of branches and sticks came showering down. He was whipped and poked by branches.

Tortoise quickly hid in his shell. After a while, there was silence.

"What have I done?" he sobbed, when the coast was clear.

The magic tree told Tortoise all that had happened. Dog had betrayed him. He was going to teach all the animals a big lesson.

That night, Tortoise couldn't sleep. His body ached. His tummy rumbled. By morning, he had a clever idea. He called all the animals together under the tree.

"I'm sorry I didn't tell you all about this magic tree. Now the tree wants to give everyone something *special*."

"Great!" the animals chorused.

Tortoise sang, but quickly hid in his shell. Branches and big sticks came showering down. All the animals were whipped and poked.

"AAAARGH!" they screamed and ran in different directions, but Tortoise was safe in his shell. Dog ran all the way to Man's village and since then, has always lived with Man.

Sunday

The Sticky Thief

One bright Sunday afternoon, the animals gathered for a meeting. A mysterious thing was happening. Someone was stealing from the animals' farm.

"I've got a clever idea," said Tortoise. "Let's keep watch every evening. An hour or two would do."

"Oh boy, that thief is going to be so sorry he messed with us!" said Buffalo.

"If I catch him, I'll swing him as far as the mountains!" shouted Monkey.

But despite their efforts, the stealing went on and on. No one could catch the thief.

"I don't understand this," complained Buffalo one evening after work. "When we keep watch on the farm, he doesn't show up. When we don't, he shows up!"

"I think it's a spirit," said Monkey. "Quite difficult to catch."

"Guys, we've worked quite hard today," said Tortoise, yawning. "Let's all go home."

The animals agreed. It had been a long day. They all went home—except Hippo, Monkey, and Buffalo.

"Enough is enough!" said Hippo. "Let's think of a better plan. Who knows, we may catch the thief."

They thought, and thought, and thought…

"Aha! A scarecrow! That could *scare* the thief," suggested Buffalo.

"What if he's strong? What if he pushes the scarecrow to the ground?" asked Monkey.

"We'll cover the scarecrow all over with sticky glue. If the thief tries to push past him, he'll get stuck," said Hippo.

"Great!" shouted Monkey.

Hippo whispered. "Let's get to work."

They collected some old rags and sticks from their shed. They made a brilliant scarecrow with dangly arms and legs. They placed it in the middle of the farm and covered it with sticky glue.

They went home, hoping the thief would come.

And he did!

Crunch, crunch! Gobble, gobble!

He walked to the middle of the farm where corn and cabbages grew. There he saw a man and panicked.

But no one scares me, he thought to himself.

"What are you doing here?" asked the thief.

There was no answer.

"All right then, get out of my way!" he said.

There was no reply.

The thief pushed him quite hard. His hand stuck!

"Let me go right now!" he demanded.

Still, there was no answer.

Then, with a mighty force, the thief pushed him even harder. His other hand got stuck too!

"Let go, let go!" he cried, kicking the man.

Both legs got stuck. He had fallen into a trap. He cried and cried until he fell asleep. The next morning, when the animals arrived at the farm, they were shocked. Stuck to the scarecrow and fast asleep snoring, was the thief—Tortoise!

"How could you?" asked Monkey, waking him up.

"You betrayed us!" yelled Hippo.

The animals were very angry.

"Let's leave him glued to the scarecrow," someone suggested.

"No, we should let him go, but he won't be working with us any longer," another said.

They tried to take him off the sticky scarecrow, but they couldn't.

"I've got an idea," said Tortoise.

"Oh, *hush!*" they chorused. "Haven't you done enough already?"

They pulled and pulled. It took a while, but in the end the animals yanked him off the sticky scarecrow. When Tortoise saw their angry faces, he became afraid and hid in his shell.

From that day onward, whenever Tortoise hears loud voices, he hides in his shell. He thinks the animals are still angry with him.

Questions

Saturday – The Magic Tree

1. Have you ever eaten so much that some of the food came out through your nose?

2. If you were Dog, what would you do about Tortoise's secret?

3. If you were Tortoise and you met Dog the next day, what might you say to him?

4. Do you think it was fair or unfair of the Magic Tree to whip Tortoise? Why?

Sunday – The Sticky Thief

1. Have you ever been in trouble for something that was your fault or wasn't even your fault?

2. What would you do if you found out that your friend did something terrible?

3. Do you agree with what the rest of the animals did to Tortoise? Why?

4. If Tortoise said, "I've learnt an important lesson today." What would that lesson be?

Use this blank page to draw your own tortoise or favourite animal.

Made in the USA
Charleston, SC
10 December 2013